301150 4290775 7

D0994939

Go to www.maxflash.co.uk,
and enter this code:
JH3OPS11LB29
for your freebies, downloads
and other Max Flash goodies

For Fiona, Jake, Ben and Isaac

STRIPES PUBLISHING
An imprint of Magi Publications
1 The Coda Centre, 189 Munster Road, London SW6 6AW

A paperback original
First published in Great Britain in 2007

Text copyright © Jonny Zucker, 2007
Illustrations copyright © Ned Woodman, 2007
Houdini photo copyright © Topfoto

The right of Jonny Zucker and Ned Woodman to be identified as the
author and illustrator of this work respectively has been asserted by
them in accordance with the Copyright, Designs and Patents Act, 1988.

ISBN-13: 978-1-84715-018-9

All rights reserved.

This book is sold subject to the condition that it shall not, by way of
trade or otherwise, be lent, resold, hired out, or otherwise circulated
without the publisher's prior consent in any form of binding or cover
other than that in which it is published and without a similar condition,
including this condition, being imposed upon the subsequent purchaser.

A CIP catalogue record for this book is available from the British Library.

Printed and bound in Belgium by Proost

2 4 6 8 10 9 7 5 3 1

MAX FLASH
MISSION 1
GAME ON

Jonny Zucker

Illustrated by
Ned Woodman

MAX FLASH
MISSION 1
CHAPTER 1

Max Flash struggled desperately with the metal
chains wrapped tightly round his upper body.
They dug into his ribs and pinched at his back.
Water gushed all around him. It was already up
to his waist and rising fast. If he didn't get out
of here in the next minute, his whole body
would be submerged.

He twisted to the left and then to the right.
One of the chains uncoiled and fell down into
the water. He allowed himself a tiny spark of
satisfaction, but still the water rose. It was now

halfway up his chest. He yanked his right elbow violently backwards and another chain came free. He tried the same move with his left elbow but the next chain remained in place. He cursed under his breath and slammed his left fist forwards and backwards until the third chain slipped off.

The water continued its rapid ascent, sweeping against his chin.

Come on, come on! Get the fourth chain off!

A sluice of water trickled into his mouth and Max spat it out violently. He shook his torso and brought his elbows crashing together, causing the final chain to disconnect. As water started to snake up his nostrils, Max reached out and grabbed the ledge above him. He dragged himself upwards, scrambling over the lip of the tank and landing on the hard wooden floorboards with a squelchy thud.

He bent double, resting the palms of his hands on his thighs, and tried to get his breath back.

"Pretty good!" nodded Max's dad, walking towards him and turning off the tap that had been flooding the tank with water. "But it was a close call. You could do with being five seconds faster."

CHAPTER 2

Max's parents Montgomery and Carly Flash
were stage magicians. They'd been performing
their magic act for over twenty years.
Montgomery's stage name was The Great
Montello, while Carly was known as Mystical
Cariba. They were both exceptionally
accomplished illusionists and their 'magic'
took in even the most hardened cynics.

Max had grown up backstage, in the wings
of theatres and arts centres, watching his
parents' performances and a host of other

magic acts. He'd been fascinated by their dazzling tricks and feats: he found out how they worked and tried them out himself. He practised and practised until he got every single one down to perfection.

But Max wasn't just good at doing magic tricks.

He had been born with a rare double-jointedness, which made his body remarkably flexible and bendy. He was the kid at school who could slide through the narrow park railings. He was the one who was never found during games of hide-and-seek because he could squeeze into the most impossibly tiny spaces.

The combination of his remarkable bodily abilities and his dedication to perfecting tricks had made him into a first class escapologist, contortionist and creator of illusions.

So being tied up in chains and escaping from a tank of water in the living room was nothing out of the ordinary. It was a new part of the stage act – based on a feat performed by Max's all-time hero Harry Houdini.

After he'd changed out of his wet clothes, Max sauntered into the living room. The tank stood in the corner, now empty of water. His parents were by the window having a hushed conversation.

"Er, excuse me," Max announced, "are you going to let me in on the secret?"

His mum and dad spun round. They both looked on edge.

"What's going on?" Max demanded.

His dad gave him a guilty-looking smile.

"There's something we need to show you," said his mum.

Max watched as they walked out of the room. His mum then unbolted the door that led down to the cellar.

He frowned.

They hardly ever went down to the cellar; it

was dark and cramped.

"Don't worry," said his dad with a reassuring smile, "it's nothing to be scared of."

As Max reached the cellar, his eyes adjusted to the dim light and he made out old tins of paint, mounds of yellowing newspapers and bits of an old motorbike strewn across the floor.

He watched his dad step over to the wooden workbench by the far wall, and feel for something behind it. To Max's utter astonishment, the workbench then began to move slowly.

It swivelled round ninety degrees and stopped when it was pressed against the cellar's left wall. His dad walked over to the space where the bench had been and slid open a floor panel.

"Er, is this part of a new trick?" asked Max, his eyes widening with surprise. "Because if it is, it looks pretty cool."

His mum shook her head. "Come and see for yourself," she said.

Max watched as first his dad and then his mum lowered themselves through the opening and began climbing down a flight of echoey metallic stairs. Max walked over and stared through the opening. It was so dark down there he could only just make out the shapes of his parents. Where did these steps lead? What exactly was down there?

He hesitated for a few seconds.

Then he took a deep breath and lowered his legs over the side.

MAX FLASH
MISSION 1
CHAPTER 3

As Max reached the bottom a row of bright ceiling lights came on and he found himself standing in a square whitewashed room about the size of his classroom. The walls were full of hi-tech silver equipment, black encased digital display panels and racks of tiny red levers and green buttons. The centrepiece of all this was a giant plasma screen in the middle of the wall facing them.

"What is this place?" Max said, scanning his surroundings. "And how long has it been here?"

"It was built before you were born," replied his dad.

"What? It's been down here my whole life and you never told me about it?"

"We couldn't," said his dad gently, "we had to wait for the right time."

His words hung in the air.

"There's someone we want you to meet," said his mum, stepping over to a row of tiny green buttons and pressing one.

In an instant the plasma screen sprang to life, revealing the face of a woman. She had piercing blue eyes, high cheekbones and thin, unsmiling lips. Her ash-blonde hair was scraped back into a tightly held ponytail.

"Good evening, Max," said the woman. "My name is Zavonne and I work for an organization called the DFEA."

Max's eyes moved from the screen to his hi-tech surroundings and over to his parents.

They gave him encouraging smiles, but this
didn't stop him feeling like his brain was about
to explode. *What* was going on down here?

"Lots of things will soon become clear to
you," said Zavonne, "but let me start by telling
you a little bit about the DFEA."

Max stared at her open-mouthed and waited
for her to go on.

"The DFEA," said Zavonne, "stands for the
Department for Extraordinary Activity. You
won't have heard of it. You won't have read
about it. You won't have seen it on TV. It is a
very, very secretive organization. The only
people who know about it are the people who
run the department and our Operatives in the
field. What I am about to tell you is highly
classified information – you are not to repeat a
single word of it to anyone outside of this
room. Do you understand?"

Max thought about this for a few seconds.
How could he agree to keep silent when he had

no idea what this strange woman was going to tell him? On the other hand it felt like she was about to share something pretty amazing with him. After all, coming through a secret door in your cellar and ending up in some sort of techno pod wasn't an everyday occurrence. Did he really want to miss out?

He nodded slowly.

"Good," replied Zavonne briskly. "The DFEA deal with 'extraordinary' matters. These are situations or events that can't be explained rationally; things that the government, the security services, the police and the army would never be able to handle."

Max looked confused. "What kind of extraordinary things?"

"Recent missions have included exorcising a road-sweeper who was possessed by the soul of the great Egyptian ruler Tutankhamen, and disabling an ambulance that kept slipping back into eighteenth-century Paris in the middle of the French Revolution."

Max burst out laughing and waited for Zavonne and his parents to join in.

But they remained silent.

Surely she wasn't being serious?

He stared into Zavonne's ice-cool eyes.

She *was* being serious.

"This is a wind-up, right?" Max asked, his voice wobbling with uncertainty. "This is being secretly filmed for some practical joke TV show or something, isn't it? It has to be."

"We know this must be very hard for you to take in," said his mum softly, "but everything Zavonne says is true. The DFEA is a real organization, doing absolutely vital work. Dad and I have carried out two major missions. That's why this communications centre is down here."

Max's mouth dropped open as he suddenly eyed his parents in a brand new light.

MISSION 1

CHAPTER 4

Missions? What was she on about? This was his mum and dad. They were stage magicians. They shopped in the supermarket. They went on camping holidays! They weren't some kind of weird undercover agents dealing with Egyptian mummies and time-travelling ambulances.

"What were the missions?" he asked.

"Ten years ago we stopped mutant sandmen from the Sahara from kidnapping the royal family," replied his mum.

"And three years ago we fought and destroyed a brigade of Tellan Warriors, who'd come from the twenty-fifth century seeking to colonize Earth," said his dad.

"Yeah, right!" said Max, his shock suddenly turning to frustration. "Next you'll be telling me we're all going to live on Mars and spend the rest of our lives eating space dust."

Zavonne's expression hardened. "I understand why this is incredibly difficult for you to believe, Max, but I can assure you that this is not some sort of game. It is deadly serious."

Max looked at his parents. "Well where was I when you fought those Tell Tale warriors or whatever they were called?"

"We hired a babysitter," replied his mum. "It was only a short battle."

Everyone was silent for a few moments and it gradually started to dawn on Max that this might actually not be some far-fetched wind-up.

In fact, with each new revelation, it was all starting to sound more and more real.

CHAPTER 5

"OK," said Max slowly, eyeing his parents. "Let's say everything I've just heard is true – why were *you* chosen for these missions?"

"Because of their magic skills," cut in Zavonne. "Your parents, as you know, are extremely experienced illusionists and escapologists. That's why they were chosen."

"But why are you telling me all this now?" Max demanded.

"Let me cut to the chase," said Zavonne. "The DFEA needs your help."

"M...m...me?" spluttered Max. "Why me?"

"You are a superb escapologist and contortionist," answered Zavonne, "plus you're a child."

"What's being a child got to do with it?"

"That will become apparent in a moment," replied Zavonne. "Let's start with the computer company, Nexus Scope. You're familiar with their games, aren't you?"

Familiar with them! Nexus Scope were the hottest gaming company in the world. Max had played loads of their games. *Centurion Warlords* and *Bogey Flickers* were his favourites.

"Our IT Unit has come across something very strange that's happening at Nexus Scope," said Zavonne. "One of their lead programmers, a man called Ricky Stevens, has just completed the prototype of a new game called *Slime Beasts of Death*."

Max raised an eyebrow.

Slime Beasts of Death?

That sounded good – lots of gooey monsters to crush and splatter!

"But there's a problem," said Zavonne. "Ricky has lost one of the characters from his game. The character's name is Deezil. He is a freak hybrid of man and lizard and is coloured red and gold."

Max frowned and mentally rewound Zavonne's statement. "What do you mean *lost*?"

"Even though Ricky has created every single micrometre of the game," Zavonne replied, "he can't locate Deezil anywhere on his hard drive."

Max stared at her in baffled silence.

"But that's only part of the problem," Zavonne added gravely. "There were two incidents in central London this morning that came to the DFEA's attention. One was in a corner shop, the other at a railway station. In each case, witnesses reported seeing a terrifying red and gold beast attacking bystanders, smashing up furniture and threatening to kill any 'Gamer' who stood in his way. Eyewitnesses were badly shaken up and the police attended both of these incidents. Fortunately, we were able to get our people to these scenes shortly afterwards. Our Operatives were able to cancel out all of the witnesses' memories of these events and all of the police officers' knowledge of them, using De-Memory Mist."

Max felt his chest tighten. "You're not trying to say that...?"

"Yes, Max," replied Zavonne. "I'm saying that Ricky Stevens has created a portal between the Virtual world and our world, or the 'Gamer' world as Deezil called it. Somehow, Deezil has located the portal and visited us. We're pretty sure he's returned to the Virtual world, but we have no idea if or when he's going to come back and what he might do if he does."

"So why don't you just get Ricky Stevens to close the portal?" said Max.

Zavonne shook her head. "Ricky has no idea that he's created this portal and we want to keep things that way. He's spooked enough about losing Deezil from *Slime Beasts of Death* and luckily hasn't told anyone about this yet. If we let him know about the portal, he'd completely freak out and within five minutes the whole planet would know about it. Can you imagine the chaos that would cause?"

"Can't the DFEA close it?" asked Max.

Zavonne sighed briefly. "We have the finest programmers on earth working for us," she replied. "They've hacked into Ricky's computer and carried out exhaustive searches of his hard drive. They are sure that the portal was created by a one in one billion accident. But so far they have not been able to close it."

She paused for a second and fixed her gaze on Max.

"I don't get it," said Max. "What do you want *me* to do?"

"We need someone to visit the Virtual world and shut the portal down, thus stopping Deezil from re-entering our world again and causing far worse trouble. And that someone, Max, is you."

Max snorted. "That's mad! Even if I believe in half of what you're saying, there's no way a human could ever visit the Virtual world! It's totally impossible!"

"Hear me out," said Zavonne, "and let me

explain my plan. In one hour Nexus Scope are
holding a special behind-the-scenes tour of
their headquarters for some winners of an
Internet competition. We've got you a ticket."

Max's pulse edged up a few gears.

A tour inside Nexus Scope? Wicked!

"You will attend this event," Zavonne
continued, "and locate Ricky Stevens' workstation. Seven USB ports on his hard drive are
being used, but the eighth one is spare. I need
you to insert something called an EP-NR USB
hub into the back of that hard drive. We've
spent years developing this hub and this will
be the first time it's ever been used. If all goes
to plan, as I'm certain it will, the second you
connect the hub you will be powered straight
inside Ricky Stevens' hard drive."

Max couldn't stifle a nervous giggle. "No
way!" he proclaimed.

"I can understand your shock," Zavonne said
briskly, "but this is an absolutely crucial

mission; there is a huge amount at stake here. If Deezil does get out again, we have no idea how much damage and chaos he could cause – it could veer out of control very quickly and cause a national emergency. We cannot let that happen, Max. Deezil must be stopped."

Max drew in some air and blew out his cheeks.

"What happens if I say no?" he asked.

"No one has ever said no to me," replied Zavonne coldly.

"I can't believe this is happening!" muttered Max, trying to process all that he had seen and heard in the last few minutes.

He turned to face his parents. "If I agree to it, can I skip my homework this weekend?"

His mum and dad glanced at each other.

They both nodded.

Max gulped nervously and turned back to Zavonne. "OK," he said, "I'll do it."

MAX FLASH
MISSION 1

CHAPTER 6

"Good," nodded Zavonne. "Now I want you to open that drawer in front of you."

A silver drawer began flashing on the wall to Max's right. He walked over and pulled it open.

This is not a dream, he told himself, *this is actually happening.*

Inside the drawer was a map, a pass for the Nexus Scope Open Day and a computer hub marked EP-NR. There was also a zip-up top, some combat trousers and a pair of sleek, new trainers.

"As you have agreed to undertake this mission," announced Zavonne, "you are now officially a DFEA Operative. You may talk to your parents about the mission but to no one else."

Max nodded his understanding as he studied the clothes, the map and the hub.

"You know what the hub is for and the Open Day pass is self-explanatory," Zavonne said. "The map contains the layout of the Nexus Scope headquarters. The *Programmers' Den* is highlighted in red. Ricky Stevens' workstation is fifth on the left."

"What's with the clothes?" asked Max. "Why can't I wear my own gear?"

"These may seem like ordinary clothes but they are far from it." Zavonne replied. "Each item is heat proof, fire proof, bullet proof, water proof and any other proof you'd care to mention. They also contain a self-cleaning mechanism, which ensures they never need to be washed."

Max's eyes lit up. A break from having to drag things to the washing basket!

"You will notice that the combats have three pockets," Zavonne went on. "In each pocket you will find a gadget. These have all been developed in top secret DFEA labs."

Gadgets?

Max loved gadgets. He and his parents used all sorts of gadgets in their stage show. He reached for the pockets and pulled out a pack of cards, a can of deodorant spray and a small pocket torch. He felt a wave of disappointment wash over him. He'd been hoping for a laser gun, something cool like that.

"The spray is a Multi-Hologram Spray," explained Zavonne. "As soon as you push the button, twenty completely realistic, life-size, 3-D versions of you will appear, confusing even the smartest opponents and buying you some time to escape, should you need it."

Max turned the spray over in his hands. *OK, that sounds pretty good.*

"The cards," continued Zavonne, "are Stair Flight Cards. Once you release them they will create a flight of steps as high in the air as you throw them. And the small pocket torch is a Universal Hole Burner. It will burn a hole in any surface. The hole will close after five seconds."

Max smiled. *Burn holes in any surface? Cool!*

"Can I try them out now?" he asked excitedly.

Zavonne shook her head. "Each gadget can only be used once. You may only use them

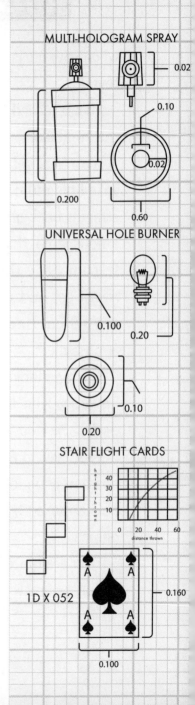

MULTI-HOLOGRAM SPRAY

UNIVERSAL HOLE BURNER

STAIR FLIGHT CARDS

when your life is in danger, Max. They are *not* toys."

Max returned the gadgets to the pockets of the combats.

"Can Max get hurt inside the hard drive?" asked his mum. "Even though Virtuals are straight back on their feet when a player starts a new game, there's no proof that they don't feel any pain. They may not get killed, but they might get hurt or be injured. Surely if Deezil can get out through the portal, then anything is possible."

Zavonne looked at the three of them impassively as Max's dad cut in. "It's a good point," he nodded. "Max will be the first Gamer ever to enter the Virtual world. We have absolutely no idea what will happen to him if he's attacked by a monster in one of the games."

"You are quite correct, we don't know if Virtual characters actually feel pain. And I can't

guarantee that Max won't get hurt." Zavonne
said.

Max saw his parents look at each other with
concern.

"This briefing is nearly over," said Zavonne. "I
won't see you again until the post-mission
debrief."

"Er, I've got a question," piped up Max.
"How do I get back? Can I use the EP-NR hub
for the return journey?"

"Everything will become clear to you when
you are on the other side, Max."

"Can't you be a little bit more specific?"
asked Max's mum. "He's our only child. We do
want him back."

Zavonne replied curtly: "I have every
confidence that Max will be able to handle any
challenges that face him. Now, if there are no
further questions, this briefing is over."

Zavonne suddenly vanished and the screen
went blank.

MAX FLASH

MISSION 1

CHAPTER 7

Max's dad pulled the car up in front of the
large iron gates of the Nexus Scope
headquarters. His mum had given him an
extra-tight hug when he'd said goodbye to her
at home before they left.

Max was wearing the DFEA clothes. They
fitted him perfectly. He felt once more for the
reassuring gadgets in the pockets of his
combats and held the map tightly in his closed
fist. In his other hand he held the pass that
Zavonne had given him for the Open Day.

"Get the job done as quickly as possible," said his dad, "and don't take any unnecessary risks."

"I'll do my best, Dad," Max replied, feeling a rush of fear and excitement.

He reached for the door handle and stepped out of the car.

Five minutes later, Max was inside the New Product Trial room, with thirty other kids. There was a row of technicians wearing silver headphones, checking out some games in progress.

The man conducting the tour of Nexus Scope had a voice that droned like an old air-conditioning unit. After a long speech about the history of the company, he turned and headed for some double doors on the far side of the room.

Max hung back, waiting for the right opportunity to split from the group. As the guide reached the double doors, Max slipped through a side door. He carefully checked the map Zavonne had given him and hurried up a flight of metal steps. He passed through a set of automatic gates, strode along a corridor and finally reached a blue door marked *Programmers' Den.*

He slowly pushed open the door and entered a space that was bursting with workstations and computers.

Max checked the map one more time and stopped at the fifth workstation on the left. Max pulled the EP-NR hub out of his top pocket, knelt down on his hands and knees and crawled under the desk. He turned the hard drive round and was faced with a bank of wires and connection points.

Thoughts and questions fizzed through his brain. *This is so unreal! It's mad! What if the hub doesn't connect properly? What if it doesn't work? What if there's a massive explosion and I'm blown to bits?*

He felt his heart thumping.

Zavonne seems to know what she's talking about, but it's me who is actually taking the risk!

Max wiped a trickle of sweat off his forehead and studied the back of the hard drive. Just as Zavonne had briefed him, there was a row of eight USB ports.

Seven had hubs connected.

One was empty.

Max took a very deep breath and pushed the hub into the empty port.

The second the hub connected to the socket, Max was surrounded by a searing flash of white light and he felt his body plummet downwards at terrifying speed.

CHAPTER 8

Max landed on his feet with a heavy thud and found himself standing in a gleaming metallic corridor that stretched as far as the eye could see in both directions. On each side of the corridor were a series of closed metal hatches.

He turned to his left and began to walk slowly down the corridor. Each metal hatch had a sign above it: *Bash the Cash, Bogey Flickers, Mutant Snake Attack, Death City Survivors*. These were all Nexus Scope games Max had played.

It's worked!

It's really worked!

I'm actually inside the hard drive of Ricky Stevens' computer! How cool is that? It isn't just some practical joke, it's the real deal! What a killer that I can't brag to any of my mates about this!

But where was the hatch leading to *Slime Beasts of Death*? It might take ages to track it down.

Ricky Stevens is a computer programmer he'll have zillions of games on his hard drive! And what if I can't find the right hatch? I don't want to get stuck in this corridor.

At that exact moment, Max spotted a hatch further down on the left.

It was half open.

But it was closing fast.

He made a split-second decision.

He sprinted forward and dived under the hatch. He rolled to a halt and stood up.

The hatch slammed shut behind him.

Max looked around. He was standing on a large strip of tarmac. He could hear the noise of cheering crowds and a deep roaring sound coming from somewhere behind him. This sound was getting louder by the second.

"GET OFF THE TRACK!" someone shouted.

Max stood up and his eyes nearly parted company with their sockets.

He was standing in the middle of a racetrack in front of a giant spectator stand bursting with an excited crowd who were cheering and clapping.

He knew this game, it was *FX Turbo Racer* –
he'd played it loads of times! It was all about
top speed, engine throttle and screeching
tyres. In the distance he could hear the roar of
the powerful, sleek cars. Max knew they could
all reach over 250 miles per hour. No wonder
Zavonne had selected him for this mission. His
parents wouldn't have a clue about any of
these games!

"I said MOVE!"

The voice was coming from a man in an
orange tracksuit who was standing behind a
meshed fence and waving his arms wildly.

Max quickly looked at the grey tarmac with its white markings. He could see sharp curves in both directions, each about a hundred metres away.

Zavonne's words flashed through his mind: *I can't guarantee that Max won't get hurt.*

He didn't want to stay on the track to test out this possibility. He spun round nervously. There was no hard shoulder or space at the side of the track in *FX Turbo Racer*, so where was he going to go?

The noise of the engines was deafening and he watched with horror as the cars hurtled round the top bend. They were now bearing down on him furiously. If he was about to be hurt, he'd be mown down ruthlessly and left with a huge tyre imprint on his face!

His heart hammered against his ribcage in panic, but he suddenly remembered the gadgets. In a split second he reached into his trouser pocket and yanked out the pack of

Stair Flight Cards. The cars were nearly upon him now – a menacing onslaught of metal force. He flicked open the lid of the pack and threw the cards in the air.

They spilt out, instantly forming a flight of steps just above the track.

Max leaped on to the first step, just before the first car thundered just a couple of centimetres below him. Quickly, he took

another couple of steps as the remaining vehicles sped beneath his body. Talk about a close shave! He was just marvelling at the genius of the cards when he and they suddenly fell down on to the track.

Max was very familiar with the track layout of *FX Turbo Racer* and he knew the cars would be round again in less than a minute. He had to act quickly.

About twenty metres up the track was a partly-concealed pit stop. Parked in this space was an empty, red car. Max heard the screech of the speeding cars pounding towards the top bend again, and he pelted towards the red car as fast he could.

CHAPTER 9

Max reached the car as the other racers took
the top bend. He grabbed the door handle and
yanked it open. To his huge relief there was a
key in the ignition. Diving on to the driver's
seat, he pulled the door shut and snapped on
the seatbelt.

He glanced in the rear-view mirror.

The other cars were nearly on him!

Frantically, he turned the key and the car
growled into life. He grabbed the steering
wheel and floored the accelerator pedal.

The car lurched forward, as the speedometer climbed from 0 to 60 in two seconds.

It was completely crazy! He was inside a *FX Turbo Racer* car!

His speed passed 100 miles an hour, then 200. He checked his mirror again. The other cars were screaming towards him, less than twenty metres away.

He remembered that a vicious bend was coming up and he gritted his teeth. As he roared round the bend at 250 miles per hour, his car spun violently on to the straight, skidding first left and then right. He had to use all of his strength on the wheel to pull the vehicle back on to the track.

But he'd lost a vital couple of seconds and a dark green car was now parallel with him on the outside of the track. Without any warning, the driver of the green vehicle suddenly pulled down hard left on his wheel and smashed into the side of Max's car.

Max cried out in shock as his car hurtled towards a huge advertising hoarding. His elbow banged against the door and he winced. That was the answer to one of his most crucial questions; he *could* feel pain in the Virtual world.

Max's mind was a blur. What was going on? *FX Turbo Racer* wasn't some violent stock car set-up. You didn't 'take out' other cars – it was an exciting but pretty straightforward, fastest-beats-all competition.

As his car bounced off a massive steel pylon at the bottom of the hoarding, he heard the sickening scrape of metal against metal and a row of sparks shot into the air.

He looked sideways. The driver of the green car was laughing like a maniac and was already turning his wheel hard for another collision.

As Max's brain frantically tried to make sense of what was happening, he spotted a yellow car scorching up on his inside. The driver of this car was also laughing with glee.

Max groaned.

Now he was going to be sandwiched between these two complete madmen.

At exactly the same second, the green and yellow drivers pulled down on their wheels, and their cars jumped sideways.

But Max was ready for them.

Thank goodness he'd played *FX Turbo Racer* so many times. He flicked the booster switch on the dashboard and instantly the red car flew forward. The green and yellow drivers realized what he'd done but they were too late. As Max powered out of their way, the other two cars crunched into each other, sending shards of glass and metal flying across the track. A couple of seconds later, the remaining vehicles smashed into the green and yellow ones. All of the cars were now tangled up and zigzagging down the track, like a twisted metal monster.

Max watched the horrific pile-up in his rear-view mirror. He didn't see the red and gold figure running across the track until the last second. He braked violently and skidded out of the figure's way.

He pushed open the door and leaped out. Had he nearly crashed into *Deezil*? He spotted the blurred figure running through an orange door beneath one of the spectator stands. Max sprinted after it, a nanosecond before the great mass of wrecked cars smashed into a giant stone wall with a sickening crash. But instead of screams coming from the drivers inside the cars, Max heard laughter and cheering. Could Deezil be somehow responsible for this new, scary anarchy?

He shuddered, turned back to the stand and sped through the orange door.

MAX FLASH
MISSION 1
CHAPTER 10

The door led into a dimly lit, narrow passageway, and as it swung shut behind him, the cheers of the *FX Turbo Racer* crowds faded to nothing. Max crept along the passage, searching all around him to see if he could get a closer look at the blurred shape he'd followed. But as he approached the end, there was an ear-splitting crash – he lost his footing and was tossed violently forward. His left shoulder took the main force of the impact and he rolled over as he hit the floor.

Opening his eyes, he looked up and the first thing he saw was an arrow heading straight for the centre of his head.

Max ducked and the arrow whistled a millimetre above him. He quickly scanned his surroundings. He was in a deep valley, dotted with clumps of trees and surrounded by ragged, brown mountains. The entire valley was heaving with thousands of Roman centurions, locked in battle.

Max knew at once that he was in *Centurion Warlords*.

Centurion Warlords was a game of strategy and quick thinking as you pitted Prince

Byzantor's army against his deadly enemy, Emperor Frelic.

But the scene in front of him was vastly different from the version he was used to. Like the drivers in *FX Turbo Racer* the centurions in the valley weren't confined to their normal fighting abilities. They were completely out of control, kicking, punching, swivelling and pirouetting.

Another arrow whizzed through the air and Max jumped out of its way. He looked at his clothes and realized he couldn't be mistaken for a Virtual. His zip-up top, combat trousers and trainers weren't exactly 'Roman'. He had to get his hands on some centurion gear, and quick!

Of course! He knew exactly where to go.

Max spun round, looked up a craggy hill and began running. He passed several mighty

sword fights and some armour-to-armour
tussling. A fireball crashed just over his head
and smashed into a large wooden gate,
throwing up a huge cloud of splinters and
flames.

Max gulped and sped on. A minute later he
ploughed into a large collection of dense
bushes. It was lucky that he knew the layout of
the game. These bushes concealed the

entrance to a secret cave that served as Prince Byzantor's armoury. Max stepped into the mouth of the cave and rounded a sharp bend.

A steely-faced man in a yellow robe was sitting behind a long oak desk, studying a piece of parchment. Behind him were rows and rows of swords and shields and maces, hanging on hooks on the cave's walls. The man looked up when he heard Max approaching.

"I am Thadius," snorted the man gruffly. "State your name!"

"Er, I'm Maximus," Max replied.

"What are those bizarre garments you wear?"

"They're, they're foreign," Max answered. "A smuggler sold them to me, but I need some armour."

Thadius eyed him contemptuously. "You're very small for a centurion," he snapped.

"True," Max agreed, "but I'm still handy with a sword."

"Listen, Maximus," the angry official hissed. "The lizard god Deezil has visited this valley and shown us that we can control our own movements in battle, and are not just at the mercy of the Gamers. For that we will be eternally grateful. But we in Prince Byzantor's army are still dedicated to fighting Emperor Frelic. The man is a tyrant and must be defeated. I suppose we need as many soldiers as we can recruit... I will find you some smaller pieces of armour."

Thadius stood up and pulled several sections of armour off hooks on the cave wall. He then reached for a huge silver shield and a long sword in a scabbard.

Max slipped the top section of body armour over his head. He then put on the bottom section and pulled on the visor with the yellow Byzantor crest. Emperor Frelic's men wore a purple crest on their visors.

Max squinted through the narrow arc of

space at the front of the helmet.

I'll be lucky if I can see my feet, let alone the hordes of Frelic's evil warlords! he thought.

"Can I ask you a question?" Max asked through the hole in his visor.

"What is it?" snapped Thadius.

"Now the centurions can control their own moves, do they feel any pain?"

Thadius eyed him suspiciously. "Of course they don't feel real pain, just like any other Virtual. Before the great lizard god appeared

we were programmed by the Gamers to bleed or die when attacked, but it was all for show. We were then forced to fall to the ground and play hurt or dead until the Gamer started up another game."

"And since Deezil arrived?" asked Max.

"We have retained the ability not to be injured or killed, only now we don't have to lie down and hang around for a Gamer to re-start the battle."

"But if you can't kill or injure each other, how is anyone ever going to win the battle?" asked Max.

"We can lock our enemies up, we can cage them, we can bind them with thick ropes!" snorted Thadius. "And that is what we intend to do with all of Frelic's men. The battle will continue! Prince Byzantor will be victorious!"

"Go Byzantor!" shouted Max, a bit too enthusiastically.

"Enough talk, mini-centurion!" thundered

Thadius. "It is high time you went into battle!"

Max clanked out of the cave and back through the bushes.

Talk about hard to walk! It's a miracle I can even stay upright!

He looked down into the valley. There was no sign of a red and gold lizard man.

If only I can track him down, I'm sure he'd lead me to that portal!

Max was halfway up a stony path, when a massive centurion suddenly blocked his way. The man's visor carried a purple crest. He was one of Frelic's soldiers and he was raising his sword high into the air.

In panic, Max held up his shield. The centurion's blade thudded against it, the impact leaving a large dent in the shield's surface.

Max's relief lasted less than a nanosecond, because Frelic's man was lifting his sword again. Max looked out of his visor in horror. As the sword reached its peak, Max swung his heavy blade against the centurion's knees with every ounce of strength he could muster. The blow was powerful enough, because it sent the centurion reeling backwards. He toppled over and crashed to the ground.

Max felt a surge of adrenaline. He hurried away from the fallen centurion, looking all around him and trying to catch a glimpse of the elusive Deezil. He'd just reached a narrow stony path when he spied one of Frelic's men on horseback, riding straight towards him. The centurion was swinging a sword.

Max looked around desperately, hearing Zavonne's words about his gadgets ringing in his ears.

You may only use them when your life is in danger.

Well his life was certainly in danger at this second but the infuriating armour meant that he couldn't get anywhere near the gadgets. The horse thundered forward and the mounted centurion swung his sword frenziedly above his head.

Please let me die without too much pain.

But when Frelic's centurion was almost upon him, a booming noise erupted in the valley.

"THIS IS YOUR LEADER, DEEZIL!"

Instantly the rider pulled up his horse, dropped the sword, dismounted and knelt on the ground. Max looked round. All over the valley, centurions were falling to their knees. Max followed suit as quickly as his armour would let him.

"A TRUCE HAS BEEN CALLED," Deezil bellowed.

There were gasps all around.

"ALL CENTURIONS MUST REPORT TO THE DUST BOWL IMMEDIATELY!"

In an instant, every centurion in the valley was marching in the direction of the dust bowl, which was situated beside Emperor Frelic's base camp. Max clanked forwards with the rest, wondering why Deezil had commanded them to stop fighting one another. The battlefield had been total chaos a moment ago, why did Deezil have the power to stop the bloodshed?

Frelic's men were gathering on the left side of the dust bowl, while Byzantor's troops were on the right. As soon as each centurion arrived, he fell on to his knees.

And at that instant, Max saw Deezil for the first time.

The lizard man was standing on top of a gigantic rock at the far side of the bowl. Up close he was truly grotesque. His top half was bright red. It had narrow sections of flesh missing that revealed hideously sharp bones protruding at every angle. His bottom half was covered in oily scales, each one dripping some sort of dark slime.

Max shuddered, and knelt down with the rest of the centurions.

"I AM HERE TO TELL YOU," roared Deezil, "THAT BEING ABLE TO CONTROL YOUR MOVEMENTS IS ONLY THE START OF MY GRAND PLAN!"

Centurions whispered amongst themselves.

"WE MUST NOW RISE UP AND BATTLE FOR OUR TOTAL FREEDOM!"

Max looked over his shoulder. Thousands more centurions were pouring into the dust bowl every second, and falling to their knees.

"YOU MUST PUT ASIDE THE HATRED THAT EXISTS BETWEEN PRINCE BYZANTOR AND EMPEROR FRELIC – FOR EVER!"

The centurions looked confused.

"GAMERS CREATED US," roared Deezil, "AND THEY *ENSLAVED* US WITH OUR LIMITED MOVES!"

"But couldn't we coexist with the Gamers?" asked one of Byzantor's men, "or ask them to grant us more moves?"

Deezil stared at the asker of this question

with fury and contempt. "THERE WILL BE NO COEXISTENCE! THE GAMERS TRAPPED US HERE. WE OWE THEM NOTHING!"

"But it's always been this way!" shouted one of Frelic's men.

"WELL IT ENDS NOW!" shrieked Deezil, hopping about with excitement. "THE GAMERS ARE OUR FOES. WE WILL FIGHT THEM ALL!"

"How can we fight them?" called out several centurions.

"A DOOR HAS OPENED BETWEEN OUR WORLD AND THEIR WORLD," hissed Deezil. "I HAVE ALREADY VISITED THE OTHER SIDE."

Gasps of shock rang throughout the valley.

"What's it like?" shouted lots of voices.

"IT'S INCREDIBLE!" shrieked Deezil maniacally. "THEY HAVE KEPT ALL OF THE GOOD THINGS FOR THEMSELVES. THEY ARE HIDEOUS, SELFISH BEINGS WHO MUST BE DESTROYED. WE NEED TO PREPARE OURSELVES FOR THE ATTACK. I WANT EVERY

SWORD SHARPENED, EVERY SHIELD CHECKED, EVERY SUIT OF ARMOUR HAMMERED INTO SHAPE. FROM THIS MOMENT ON, YOU WILL NOT RAISE YOUR WEAPONS AGAINST EACH OTHER. YOU ARE NOW ON THE *SAME SIDE*!"

There was dead silence in the valley for a second and then suddenly a spontaneous outbreak of cheering and shouting erupted. Centurions from opposite sides were suddenly shaking hands and hugging each other as best as they could through the heavy suits of armour.

Max felt his throat tighten.

This was way beyond scary. Deezil wasn't just some day-tripper, happy to visit the Gamers' world and carry on with his life in the Virtual world. No, his plan was obvious now; Deezil intended to lead all of the characters from the Virtual world through the portal to take on the Gamers.

The very future of humanity was at stake!

And Max was the only person who could stop him.

I mustn't let the lizard man out of my sight. When all of the Virtuals are ready for the battle, Deezil will have to return to Slime Beasts and the portal. So long as I stick close to him, he'll lead me there. And when I finally reach the portal, I must stop him or any of his fellow Virtuals getting through.

Max's attention was brought back to Deezil. "ENOUGH!" shouted the lizard man.

There was immediate silence in the dust bowl.

He paused for a few seconds.

"WE WILL FIGHT THE GAMERS AND WE WILL DEFEAT THEM!"

Another colossal bout of cheering and clapping exploded.

Don't take your eyes off Deezil, Max's brain urged him.

But a second later, a great chinking of metal sounded, as the centurions rose to their feet and headed back to their bases, to prepare for the ensuing battle against the Gamers. Max suddenly found himself being swept up in the vast crowd as it herded its way back out of the dust bowl. Max wriggled furiously as he was dragged along.

"Let me go," he shouted. "I have to get back there."

But the force of the crowd was immense. Max glanced round and saw Deezil leaping down from the rock and holding an intense conversation with several centurions.

"Please!" screamed Max. "You have to let me go!"

But his cries were ignored as the mass of bodies pulled him on.

And with every step, he was being taken further and further away from the evil lizard man.

CHAPTER 13

It was ten minutes later that Max finally
managed to break away from the thick mass of
movement and make his way back to the
gigantic rock in the dust bowl. To his despair,
all traces of Deezil had gone.

He hurried out of the bowl and began to
scour the valley. Everywhere, centurions were
working industriously on battle preparations,
just as Deezil had commanded. It was so weird
seeing Frelic's men and Byzantor's men sitting
together, sharpening their sword blades,

banging dented pieces of armour back into shape and sharing battle stories and jokes.

He stopped several times to ask groups of centurions if they'd seen Deezil or if they knew where he could find *Slime Beasts of Death* and the portal, but none of them had a clue. After a fruitless hour of searching, Max found himself back at the armoury cave. Thadius was still seated behind his desk, but he'd brightened up a bit and was now only scowling rather than shouting.

"You again?" said Thadius.

"Me again," smiled Max weakly.

"Make yourself useful," Thadius said. "Go and give Savasha a hand. She's a Barbarian slave and I warn you, she has a loose tongue."

Max glanced over and spotted a young woman scraping a piece of stone against a metal blade and muttering angrily under her breath. Savasha looked about eighteen, with long, flowing blonde hair and emerald-green eyes.

"Can I help you?" asked Max, walking over to her.

She looked up and, on seeing Max, spat on the floor.

"You're pathetic," she hissed. "Every one of you! Curse Emperor Frelic and curse Prince Byzantor!"

"Hi, I'm Max, er I mean, Maximus," he smiled, trying to win her over with his charm.

She spat on the ground again and held her stone still for a moment. "All it took was that creature Deezil to shout at you and you all stopped

fighting!" she snarled. "Call yourselves *men*?"

"But didn't you hear what he said about rising up against the Gamers?" Max asked.

"Pah!" snorted Savasha. "What happens if the Virtuals lose that particular battle, huh? The Gamers could make all of us their slaves. Conditions on the other side could be worse than here!"

"So what are you going to do when the battle begins?" Max asked.

Savasha threw her head back and laughed. "You think I'd tell you? Some half-sized excuse for a Byzantor centurion!"

"Hang on," replied Max, a little offended, "I may be small but I can tell you that things aren't always what they seem."

He hurried round the bend to the front of the cave and took off his centurion gear. Thadius was too engrossed with a piece of parchment to notice what he was doing. When Max reappeared Savasha eyed him with shock.

"What have you done with your armour?"she asked.

"If you help me," he told her, "I'll make sure you escape from the clutches of these centurion warlords."

Savasha stared at him in surprise. "How can you make such a promise! You're a Virtual just like the rest of us."

"No, Savasha," Max replied coolly, "I'm a *Gamer*."

"Fascinating!" crowed a third voice.

Max and Savasha spun round.

Standing behind them was Deezil, with a large group of fierce-looking centurions.

"We have a Gamer spy in our midst," growled Deezil, staring at Max with a hideous grin. "This Gamer can only be in our world for one reason! He is here to sabotage my plan! He intends to stop us crossing over to his world!"

"What do you want us to do with him?" asked another of the centurions.

Deezil stuck out his tongue and rolled it across his lips. It was forked and green and coated with disgusting yellow slime.

"Kill him," he hissed.

CHAPTER 14

At that second, Max remembered the perfect gadget to aid his escape.

Multi-Hologram Spray!

He grabbed the can from the pocket of his combats and squeezed a powerful blast into the air. Twenty life-sized 3-D images of him were projected all over the cave. Deezil and the centurions looked around completely bewildered. The real Max smiled as he turned and fled into the tunnel that led into the depths of the cave.

The tunnel was very dark, its only light coming from a faint glow in the distance. It smelt of damp and moss. Drips of water plopped on to Max's head every few metres. The tunnel led downwards. As he fled, Max's mind fizzed with questions. Would the tunnel lead to a possible escape route? Might it take him a step nearer to *Slime Beasts of Death* and the portal? Or would it be a dead end – enabling Deezil's men to trap him and kill him? The Multi-Hologram Spray had bought him a minute or two, but he could hear heavy footsteps pounding mercilessly after him.

"THIS WAY!"

It was Deezil's voice.

"HURRY UP! THAT REVOLTING LITTLE GAMER COULD STAND BETWEEN US AND FREEDOM!"

Max sped up, almost tumbling as his trainers crashed over pebbles and boulders.

"THERE HE IS!" shrieked Deezil.

Max looked over his shoulder. He could see

dark shapes in hot pursuit and the clang of metal swords bouncing off the tunnel walls. He was approaching the light now and could see that it was created by a hole in the tunnel roof. Just beneath this was a crossroads, with three gloomy paths.

Which should I take? The left one, the middle one or the right one?

He knew that a wrong decision could cost him his life.

Which one? WHICH ONE?

He'd just decided on the left path, when something suddenly caught his eye.

"FASTER!" screamed Deezil as he hurtled forwards and reached the crossroads, with the centurions right behind him. "WHERE IS HE?" screamed Deezil.

The centurions looked around but there was no sign of the boy.

"FIND HIM!"

Deezil banged his right fist into the palm of

his left hand. "He must be here somewhere!"

His voice echoed off the damp walls.

"There's no sign of him," called out a centurion.

"Right," snarled Deezil. "I want three of you to take the left path, three of you to take the right path and the rest to take the middle path with me."

The crunching footsteps took off again and after a couple of minutes, the noise faded away.

Max breathed a huge sigh of relief as he slipped out of the very narrow crack into which he'd just managed to squeeze and hide himself, a second before Deezil and the centurions arrived at the crossroads. He'd watched them appear and held his breath as they searched for him. He'd then seen them run off to continue their search. Max brushed the dust and cobwebs off his zip-up top and stayed still for a minute, thinking about Deezil's plan.

OK. Deezil was preparing all of the Virtuals on Ricky Stevens' hard drive to get through the portal and battle the Gamers. How many Virtuals could there be on Ricky's hard drive? Just think about all of the centurions in *Centurion Warlords*, there were easily tens of thousands of them, and that was only one game. If every character in every game joined the Virtual army, it could probably stretch to millions.

And it wasn't like the Gamers would have more sophisticated weapons than the Virtuals – it was the other way round! Computer programmers had unwittingly armed Virtuals with the most destructive methods of attack. The combined might of the Gamers' police, army, air-force and navy would surely be no match for the Ubez People from *Flight of Pain*, who had limitless stocks of nuclear rocket launchers? And what about the giant Mutant Ants from *Cloud Catastrophe*? They would use low-flying drone planes to spread their Deadly Butt Mist and suffocate everything in its path.

The Gamers would get mashed!

Max stepped into the left tunnel and hurried along it. About seventy metres down on the right, he spied a wooden stable door with two halves. From beyond the door he could hear the muted sound of thumping country and western music.

Max hated country and western music almost as much as he hated homework, but surely it was better than hanging around for Deezil and the centurions to catch him?

CHAPTER 15

Max pushed on the top half of the door but it didn't budge. He had no luck with the bottom half either. He gave the door a barge with his shoulder . . . still nothing. Standing back, he aimed a high kick at the centre of the door and both halves flew open. As he sprang forwards, the music flooded into his ears.

It was *Yankee Doodle*, with a thumping bass and crashing beat.

Max's eyes adjusted to the light and he saw he was in a lush green meadow, with fluffy sheep grazing all around him at the bottom of a gently rising hill. He couldn't see Deezil or any centurions, so that was a good start. A skinny girl with plaits in her hair, dazzling blue eyes and wearing a frilly dress, suddenly appeared at his side and linked her arm through his.

"Hi there, cowboy!" she yelled with an American twang. "I'm Daisy Do-Good! Welcome to *Farmyard Frolics*!"

Before Max could reply, Daisy skipped off up the hill of the meadow. Because their arms were linked, Max had no choice other than skip with her.

Max was so grateful that his mates couldn't see him now! They would howl with laughter at his humiliation. It would catapult him straight to the top of the embarrassment charts. He'd never be able to live it down!

Max knew all about Daisy Do-Good and *Farmyard Frolics*. He'd seen one of his mates' little sisters playing it. As far as he'd been able to tell, the sole aim of the game was to create the world's tidiest and most organized farm.

That wasn't a proper game! Where was the combat? Where were the weapons?

"It's real crazy today," Daisy shouted as they neared the brow of a hill. "We're rounding folks up for the big battle against those nasty Gamer critters. Mr Deezil has got us all organized."

"Wait," urged Max. "This is all a terrible mistake. You can't go to war!"

"Say *what*?" asked Daisy, letting go of his arm and giving him a funny look.

"It'll be a disaster," hissed Max. "Loads of Virtuals and Gamers will be killed. Please, Daisy! You've got to trust me! Do you know where Deezil is or how I can get into *Slime Beasts of Death*?"

"What the heck is goin' on?" shouted a gruff old man, with white hair and a straggly white beard, who was striding towards them carrying a pitchfork.

"This boy says the battle might not be such a good idea, Pa," replied Daisy. "Reckons Mr Deezil is up to no good."

The man eyed Max with contempt.

"Mr Deezil's just sent word that there's a Gamer kid on the loose, trying to stop us getting through that portal," hissed Pa. "This must be him!"

"Oh my!" gasped Daisy in shock.

Pa nudged Max on the shoulder with his pitchfork.

"I know what I'm talking about," said Max

quickly. "Deezil, I mean, *Mr Deezil*, is a mad man or mad lizard or, whatever, he's just . . . *mad*. He's leading you into all sorts of dangers and he–"

"BUTTON IT!" cut in Pa. "Since Mr Deezil entered our lives, we've been able to control our own moves and make this farm tidier and more organized than it's ever been before. And Mr Deezil has told us all about the Gamers' world. Do you really think we're just gonna sit here and turn down this opportunity? We're on our way and there's nothing you can do to stop us! You and your Gamer buddies are welcome to the farm and everything else."

Max stared at Pa.

"What did you just say?" he asked.

"He said the Gamers are welcome to the farm and everything else," replied Daisy, helpfully.

Max felt as if several million light bulbs had just exploded inside his brain.

Why hadn't he seen it earlier?

Deezil doesn't just want to take the Gamers on. He wants to swap places with them. While the lizard man and his fellow Virtuals took over the Gamer world, the Gamers would be shoved into the Virtual world and forced to live here for ever.

He had to get away from Pa and Farmyard Frolics, and find Deezil!

Max turned and started speeding up the hill. He flew forwards and reached the brow of the hill in less than fifteen seconds. As he hit the peak, he glanced back over his shoulder. He was horrified to see Pa and a large gang of beefy farm workers running after him, yelling

at the top of their voices and waving pitchforks furiously. Max sped down the other side of the hill. Up ahead was the farmhouse, with a decked porch the whole way round it.

In absolute desperation, Max flew inside and dived through the first door he came to. He found himself whooshing through the air, and realized he must have stumbled across an entrance into another game. Suddenly, he was crashing through leaves, and found himself hanging on to a tree branch, about thirty metres above the ground. Surrounding him were hundreds of other thick trees, their branches stretching out in all directions. The air was hot and sticky. But of more immediate concern was the massive, drooling, slimy lime green creature that was shaking the bottom of Max's tree and laughing like a maniac.

CHAPTER 16

Max gulped with terror as he stared down at the beast below. On the plus side, it looked like he'd finally arrived in *Slime Beasts of Death*. On the minus side, the hideous creature was now climbing the tree.

Max tried to keep calm, but he knew that facing this monster would be his hardest challenge. He'd known lots about all of the other games he'd visited and this had really helped him. But he knew absolutely nothing about the layout or character powers in *Slime Beasts*.

It was a prototype.

The only person who'd ever played it was Ricky Stevens.

Max cursed the Nexus Scope computer programmer. If it hadn't been for him accidentally creating the stupid portal, Max would be safe at home now and not facing a potentially slimy death.

The vile beast was within touching distance now and it reached out a disgustingly oily arm. Max kicked it off, but it grabbed him with its other arm.

Max kicked out again, but the creature prised him away from the trunk and the two of them fell crashing to the ground.

Luckily for Max, they landed on a thick dry bush and bounced forward on to a pool of caked earth. Max untangled himself from the monster's grip and sprung away from the bush. He swerved round and came-face-to-face with the beast.

On the ground it looked even more horrific. It was well over two metres tall and its gigantic hairy body was covered in oozing yellow spots. Its three mouths were overcrowded with hundreds of red teeth and it had six bloodshot eyes. Max looked around to see if there were any other disgusting creatures in the vicinity, but he and the monster appeared to be alone.

"So you must be the Gamer boy!" hissed the beast, eyeing Max as huge globs of black drool slid out of his mouth. "Deezil warned us about you. He said if we found you, we should eat you."

"I'd taste disgusting," shouted Max. "There's hardly any meat on me. I'm all bones."

Three fat and furry tongues slid out of three repulsive mouths.

"I LOVE bones," hissed the creature.

"OK then," cried Max, "maybe, maybe I can help you with with your teeth."

"MY TEETH?" it roared.

"Yeah," Max nodded vigorously. "I know this great orthodontist. She could fit you with some braces to really sort out those mouths of yours."

The beast let out a low, angry growl and made a swoop for Max.

Max darted out of its way.

It twisted round and stamped towards him.

"OK," Max screamed. "We'll leave the braces, she could just do a shine and polish!"

The monster loomed over Max and lowered its head until it was only a few centimetres from Max's face. Its breath smelt of engine oil and rotting cabbages and close up its skin was slimy and oozing pus.

"She also does tooth whitening," yelled Max in desperation, taking two more large steps backwards.

Suddenly he felt his back come up against a solid tree trunk.

The monster reached out its left hand and grabbed Max by the neck.

"At last," it cackled. "Time for my meal!"

As the creature lifted him hungrily towards its lips, Max sunk his teeth into one of its cheeks.

"AAAAAAAARRRRRRRRRRGGGGHHHHHHH!" shrieked the monster, releasing Max from its grasp and sending him crashing to the ground. Two of its zits exploded in a shower of yellow pus. A large splat landed on Max's head.

Euuuuurgghh! Disgusting.

The creature was now lying on the jungle floor, howling in pain and holding its cheek in agony.

Max didn't hang around – he ran down a narrow track, leaped over a stream overflowing with bubbling slime and criss-crossed between some trees, the air sticky and hot all around him.

I'm in Slime Beasts. The portal is somewhere in this game. If I find it I might be able to close it. I have to stop Deezil's vile plan.

He tumbled into a small clearing, panting and drenched in sweat.

But before he could get back into his stride, he heard a terrific slam and felt metal chains being wrapped tightly round his body.

Max saw at once that he was inside a small barred cage. He'd been tricked!

"I think this little game of yours is over!" hissed Deezil.

CHAPTER 17

"It's only just begun," snarled Max defiantly, through the bars of the cage.

"Oh no it hasn't," roared Deezil.

"Oh yes it..."

Max stopped himself from getting into pantomime mode. The situation was far too serious for comedy banter.

He shook his body, but there was almost no give in the chains.

Deezil laughed at his struggles but then a ferocious scowl suddenly appeared on his face.

"I am sick and tired of you running round this hard drive trying to unsettle my troops and stand in the way of my glorious plan."

"It's *not* glorious," yelled back Max. "It's madness! You have no idea about what will happen to you and the Virtuals on the other side."

"I HAVE BEEN THERE!" bellowed Deezil.

"Yeah, for one hour," Max pointed out. "If you think it will be a straightforward battle you're totally deluded. You could get all of your Virtual mates destroyed."

"I will not listen to you. The time has come to lead my people through the portal."

"NO!" Max pleaded. "You mustn't do it, the fallout will be gigantic!"

But Deezil wasn't prepared to listen to another word. He pulled out a silver microphone that was inside a small pack resting over his shoulder and switched it on.

"COMRADES! YOU MUST ALL GATHER NOW

BY THE PORTAL. THE TIME FOR BATTLE HAS FINALLY COME!"

And with that, Deezil grabbed the long handle in front of the cage and started wheeling it forwards. Max tried the chains again.

There was no give.

It was finally over. He'd have to spend the rest of his life as a prisoner in the hard drive. He had to do something!

Deezil pulled Max along in the tiny cage through the moist jungle air and the vast thicket of trees. When they finally emerged from the trees, Max saw they were in a huge, dried-mud field.

At the far side of the field, in between two slimy pools of sticky green lava, was an opening, hovering in the air. It was the height and width of a regular door in the Gamers' world. At last – the portal!

CHAPTER 18

"In a few moments," Deezil declared, his chest swelling with pride, "I will go streaming through that portal, along with my fellow Virtuals. Millions and millions of us. And you will be left here, a powerless spectator to such a triumphant occasion." He cackled with laughter. "Just think!" he cried. "In a short while, you will be reunited with all of your filthy Gamer pals!"

Deezil grabbed the cage handle and started pulling it across the field.

In the background, Max could hear the rising noise of marching feet and cries of celebration. He turned round as far as he could and saw shapes emerging from the trees.

It was the rest of the Virtuals!

There were the drivers from *FX Turbo Racer*; the Gargons plus hundreds of other aliens from *Space Rage*; countless centurions from Byzantor's and Frelic's armies; Savasha the Barbarian slave being nudged forward by Thadius and not looking very happy about this; Daisy Do-Good, Pa and a gang of farm hands, travelling in the yellow truck; hundreds of gruesome slime beasts; a large posse of cobras from *Mutant Snake Attack*; the Greenheads from *Bogey Flickers*; the armed vigilantes from *Bash the Cash*; the chrome-clad bikers from *Death City Survival* and thousands and thousands more.

It was a truly scary sight.

Deezil was hopping with glee.

"KEEP MOVING!" he cried to the Virtual army. "KEEP MOVING!"

Max gulped nervously.

The field was rapidly filling up with Virtuals and thousands were still pouring out from the trees.

Max kicked his leg in frustration against the bars of the cage. As he did so, he felt a movement in one of the chains and the tip of his left elbow was suddenly free. He quickly looked at Deezil to see if he'd noticed. But the lizard man was jumping about with delight, calling greetings and urging the Virtuals to hurry up.

He thought back to his water tank practice in the living room with Dad, and about the countless hours he'd spent honing his skills.

He was Max Flash, wasn't he? Master escapologist! He could do this!

He thrust his elbow backwards with a violent push and a chain slipped off his shoulder. He

wriggled his shoulder backwards and forwards in quick succession and another chain came loose. He now had momentum and after several tugs and twists and turns, he was free. Max tried to squeeze an elbow between the cage's bars, but he didn't have enough room to angle it through.

The lizard man was less than twenty metres away from the portal, when he suddenly let out a ferocious scream.

The portal was starting to close.

CHAPTER 19

Max eyed it with absolute astonishment. Why was this happening? *How* was it happening?

Deezil rounded violently on Max.

"THIS IS YOUR DOING!" he screamed.

"I wish it was," shouted Max, "but it's not me."

And at that very second, strange things began happening all over the field.

The Virtuals had frozen in their tracks and were starting to move in straight plains and arcs. Some were walking backwards, others

were crashing into each other; some were raising their arms repeatedly in the air; others were running back to the trees in speedy, robotic moves.

Max realized instantly what was happening.

The open portal had enabled the Virtuals to control their own movements. But as the portal was closing now, these powers were obviously being taken away. They were being dragged away from the portal, most probably to their 'home' games.

But who had de-activated the portal? It wasn't me, and it obviously wasn't Deezil.

They were now all moving in the ways that Max had always seen, the ways that Ricky Stevens and the other Nexus Scope programmers had designed. They weren't going to make it through the portal. But the same couldn't be said for Deezil.

The lizard man had dropped the handle that was pulling the cage and was desperately fighting the force that was tugging him away from the portal. And even though it was clearly a terrible struggle for him, he was taking small steps towards the portal. He was only about ten metres away.

Max panicked.

OK, the Virtuals weren't going to get through the portal – this was good.

But Deezil was a determined madman and he was nearly there – this was bad – this was *very* bad.

What would Harry Houdini do in a situation like this? *Think!* Max crashed his body backwards and managed to get his right hand through one of the bars. He followed this with his right shoulder and then eased his head through. Next he collapsed his body to make it as thin as was humanly possible, and began to feed first his chest, then his stomach through.

He glanced up.

Deezil was straining every sinew in his body

and was now less than five metres away from the portal. A couple more steps and he'd be through.

Max gritted his teeth and with a tremendous push, forced his waist through the bars, followed by his legs and finally his feet.

Deezil was now less than a metre away from the portal. In an instant he'd be through, and it would be game over for Max.

I must stop him!

MAX FLASH
MISSION 1
CHAPTER 20

Max sprinted forward and jumped in front of
the portal, blocking Deezil's way. The lizard
man howled with rage and tried to take a
swipe at Max, who held up his arms to deflect
the blow. But none came. Deezil's movements
spluttered to a halt, his sharp nails inches from
Max's face. Max eyed the portal: he calculated
that he had no more than 5 minutes before it
closed completely. He hurled Deezil into the
cage, and dragged him back through the trees.
Up ahead, he could see enormous lines of

Virtuals moving through a hatch next to a
rocky waterfall.

Max spotted the grotesque creature who'd
attacked him. It was settling itself down into a
giant mud bath, and the other Slime Beasts
were wandering off to their regular hangouts.

"WHERE ARE YOU TAKING ME?" shrieked
Deezil. "Put me down here, in my own game. I
promise you that I'll stay in *Slime Beasts of
Death* and never trouble you again."

"Interesting offer," nodded Max, "but I'm
afraid the answer's NO."

As Max strode through the hatch, he found
himself back in the long gleaming corridor he'd
landed in when he first arrived inside Ricky
Stevens' hard drive.

As far as the eye could see, massive numbers
of Virtuals were moving up the corridor and
disappearing through open hatches, returning
to their own games.

When a complete set of Virtuals had

returned to their game, the hatch of that game slammed shut.

The entire corridor rang out with footsteps and the clanging of hatches closing.

"Where are you taking me?" asked Deezil in terror.

"Relax," smiled Max, "you're going to love it there."

Max rushed on down the corridor, studying the signs above each hatch and very wary that

the portal was closing by the second.

He finally reached the sign he was looking for.

Deezil stared in horror at the sign. "No," he choked. "Please! Anywhere but here! I'm BEGGING YOU!"

The hatch for this game was already closed.

"You see," shouted Deezil. "You can't stick me in there! You'll have to return me to my home game."

Max reached into the pocket of his combats and pulled out the Universal Hole Burner. He shone it against the hatch and with a fizzing sound, an opening suddenly appeared.

"Have fun," grinned Max, as he pulled Deezil out of the cage and flung him through the hole.

"NNNNNNNOOOOOOOOOOOOOOOOO!!" screamed Deezil as he flew through the air.

A split second later, the hole had closed up again and Deezil's fate was sealed.

But there was no time for celebrations. Soon that portal would be closed, and he'd be stuck here for ever!

Max sped back through the hatch leading to *Slime Beasts of Death* and hurtled through the undergrowth.

Please let the portal still be open!

Finally he reached the end of the trees. He pelted out into the field and saw to his horror that the portal was almost closed.

He thundered across the field, his mind working frantically on the proportions of the portal. There was now absolutely no way he'd be able to fit his whole body through the gap.

It would require something very special, a skill only he possessed.

As he crashed forward, he tucked his chin right down towards his chest and wrapped up his body, transforming himself into a human bowling ball. He closed his eyes and spun forward and to his amazement, he felt his body

crash against the sides of the portal and fly beyond it.

Immediately, he heard a gigantic swooshing sound as the portal sealed upbehind him.

He'd just made it.

He was back.

CHAPTER 21

Max found himself lying on the floor of a
gloomy tunnel, where a rat was eyeing him
with interest. He looked all around him. There
was no sign of the portal anywhere.

To his left was a long metal ladder that
stretched up towards a thin shaft of pale
yellow light. Stay down here and spend some
quality time with an inquisitive rodent or climb
the ladder?

It wasn't a difficult decision.

At the top of the ladder, he discovered the

underside of a manhole. Using both hands he
pushed it upwards and to the left. He eased
himself out and a car wildly swerved out of his
way, one of its wheels narrowly missing his
head.

For a second he feared that he was still in
the Virtual world and that this was *FX Turbo*

Racer. But when he poked his head up, he saw he was bang in the middle of a very busy road – a very busy Gamer road.

A large bus bore down on him. Max rolled out of its way and reached the pavement. He stood up and dusted himself down.

"Where did you appear from?"

Max came face-to-face with a lanky policeman with thin lips and bushy eyebrows.

"From that manhole over there," Max replied, pointing to the middle of the road.

The policeman frowned. "Are you trying to be funny?" he asked.

Max turned round.

There was no sign of the manhole.

"So, where have you been?" asked the officer, leaning suspiciously towards him.

"It's complicated," replied Max cautiously, "but I won't be going there again."

"And why is that then?"

"It was incredibly hard getting back from there – in fact it was *virtually* impossible."

And with that Max flashed his cheesiest-school-photograph-smile and hurried off down the street. He hadn't got far when a blur of red and gold suddenly flashed before his eyes.

CHAPTER 22

Max felt every muscle in his body tense, but laughed out loud when he saw that the red and gold was simply a leaf that had fallen from a tree on to the pavement. Two women pushing prams saw him laughing at a leaf and began whispering to each other and giving him strange looks. He walked on.

"Max!" cried his mum when she opened the front door. She smothered him in an enormous hug. His dad ran out of the kitchen with a wide grin on his face.

"What a relief," whispered Dad, placing a strong arm round his son's shoulders.

"It's so good to be back," grinned Max.

"We want to hear all about it," beamed Mum, "but first you need to have your debrief with Zavonne."

His dad accompanied him down to the cellar, moved the workbench and opened up the floor panel.

"Aren't you coming in with me?" asked Max.

His dad shook his head. "It was fine for us to be with you on the initial brief, but now you're a fully-fledged Operative, you must meet with Zavonne on your own."

Max shrugged his shoulders. "Cool," he nodded.

"Good," smiled his dad. "Have the debrief, then come and tell us everything."

Max hurried down to the cellar. He couldn't wait for Zavonne to applaud his efforts. Maybe she'd give him a reward, like a brand new computer with every Nexus Scope game?

Thirty seconds later Max was back in the communications centre.

He pressed the green button he'd observed his mum activating when he first came down here, and the plasma screen sprang into life.

Zavonne's face appeared.

Max waited to be showered in praise.

"What took you so long?" Zavonne demanded.

Max frowned. Was she joking? He'd just saved the human race from being caged inside the Virtual world and she was being picky about his timekeeping?

"I did it as fast as I could," he replied defensively.

"I take it you used all three gadgets?" asked Zavonne.

Max nodded.

Zavonne tutted.

"I only used them when my life was in danger," Max replied.

This was true apart from using the Universal Hole Burner on the hatch, but how would Zavonne ever know that?

"On balance," she noted coldly, "your first mission was satisfactory."

Satisfactory? Was that the best she could do?

"I have a question," Max said.

Zavonne nodded.

"How did the portal close?"

Zavonne looked back at him coolly. "Our IT people finally found a way of doing it."

Max stared back at her in horror.

"But I was still in there!"

"It was a risk we had to take."

But even as she was saying this, something else occurred to Max. "Hang on a second," he said, his voice rising several decibels. "I think I've just worked out what EP-NR stands for – the letters on the hub for Ricky's hard drive."

Zavonne stared at him without expression.

"It's ENTRY POINT – NO RETURN, isn't it?" said Max. "It *must* be. You sent me there on a one way ticket!"

"Yes," conceded Zavonne. "That is what the letters stand for. But I had absolute faith in you. I knew that you would be able to make your way back to our world. That's why I sanctioned the use of the EP-NR hub and that's why I gave the go-ahead for our people to close

down the portal."

Max was absolutely stunned.

Zavonne had taken huge risks with his life yet it didn't seem to faze her at all. Zavonne was unreal. She couldn't be human. She possessed the emotions of an ice sculpture.

"Right then," said Zavonne, "this debrief is over and–"

"Hang on a sec," blurted out Max. "What about the future? How do you know Ricky Stevens or some other programmer isn't going to accidentally create another portal?"

Zavonne looked at Max impatiently. "It was, as I told you, a one in one billion accident. It will not happen again. And anyway, we now have the technical knowledge of how to close portals."

Max would have liked to ask her some more questions but Zavonne quickly spoke again. "Our paths may well meet again, Max," she said, giving him a thin impenetrable smile that was harder to crack than the Mona Lisa's, and then her face suddenly vanished from the screen.

Max's parents were waiting upstairs for him in the kitchen.

"We can't wait to hear about the mission," said his mum, "but first you have to take a bath, you're absolutely filthy."

"I can't be," protested Max, "the DFEA clothes are self-cleaning. You heard what Zavonne said."

"It's not the clothes," laughed his dad. "It's your face. And what is that disgusting stuff in your hair?"

"Oh that," sighed Max. "It's probably Slime Beast drool."

He sped upstairs to the bathroom.

Typical!

He'd just saved the entire human race and here were his parents treating him like a kid again!

EPILOGUE

Ricky Stevens had spent much of the weekend thinking about Deezil's disappearance from *Slime Beasts of Death*. He got to work early on Monday morning, determined to get to the bottom of the mystery. But as he entered the *Programmers' Den*, his boss asked him to take a look at *Farmyard Frolics*. She wanted to get his ideas about new features for the second version of the game.

Ricky grimaced. *Farmyard Frolics* wasn't a 'real' game in his eyes, but it was best to keep his boss happy. So he slid down on to his chair, flicked on his computer, and opened *Farmyard Frolics* on his hard drive.

As the game loaded and the wide-angle shot of the farm appeared, Ricky was stunned by what he saw.

There, down on the farm, was Daisy Do-Good supervising one of her workers, whose job it was to go around the farm picking up the sheep droppings and loading them into a giant bin bag. The worker was covered from head to toe in sheep dung.

The worker was Deezil.

Ricky was just about to remove Deezil from the farm and put him back in his rightful place in *Slime Beasts of Death*, when he paused and laughed out loud. Deezil looked so miserable, maybe he'd leave him on the farm as punishment for his disappearing act. A few hours with dippy Daisy would tame even the most fearsome of lizard men.

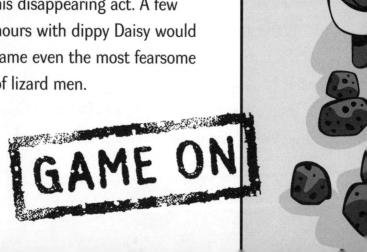

GAME ON

Go to www.maxflash.co.uk,
and enter this code:
JH3OPS11LB29
for your freebies, downloads
and other Max Flash goodies

Major thanks to
Jane Harris and
Lauren Buckland
for their massive
roles in creating Max
and their supreme
editing skills,
Monty Bhatia
for totally backing
this project from
the start,
Janice Swanson
for getting me in
on the 'ground floor'
and
Steph Thwaites
for always
being on the case.

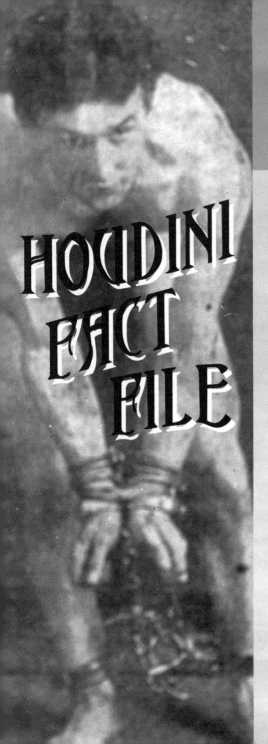

HOUDINI FACT FILE

Max's escape from a tank of water was based on one of Harry Houdini's most famous acts. This was known as the Chinese Water Torture Cell and was first performed in 1913. The set up for this feat was in four stages: Houdini's feet were locked in stocks. He was suspended in mid air from his ankles and had a restraint brace (similar to a straight jacket) fixed over his body. He was lowered head first into a steel and glass tank, known as a 'Cell' that was completely filled with

THE CHINESE WATER TORTURE CELL

water. The restraint brace was locked to the roof of the
cell and the cell lid was locked shut. As soon as the lid
was closed, a curtain was pulled across in front of the
cell so that the audience couldn't see what Houdini
was doing, and loud music was played so they couldn't
hear anything. Houdini was a master at keeping his
escape methods a secret, but magic experts insist they
know how he got out. They say that:

Crucially, Houdini could hold his breath for 3 minutes
(a feat that should NEVER be tried except by the
world's top escapologists). To escape from the cell,
Houdini had to unlock the stocks and the lock tying
his brace to the roof of the tank. To do this he used a
tiny key. This was either hidden in a miniscule,
impossible-to-spot pocket in the restraint brace or he'd
swallowed a key and regurgitated it once inside the cell
(urgh!). To lose the brace, Houdini used a special
technique where he puffed out his shoulders and chest
and then suddenly twisted his shoulders and wriggled
free. As for the cell's lid, this either had a false panel;
or it contained a secret lock – that key came in handy
for this of course! Houdini then climbed out of the cell
and pulled the curtain aside. He was drenched in water
but alive, and audiences all over the world went
completely wild!

MONSTER SIGHTED - OPINIONS WANTED!

posted by Coda:

Seventy-year-old Horace Winthrop has
contacted us with a very suspicious story.
Mr Winthrop was waiting for his grandson
at Waterloo Station yesterday morning when
he asserts that he was attacked by a terrifying
red and gold lizard creature. There was total
chaos as everyone tried to escape from the
beast, which vanished when the police arrived.
Not an every day occurrence, that's for sure.
A vicious monster causing carnage would be
front page news. Right? But there has been
NO mention of this incident and there appear
to be no other witnesses.
Mr Winthrop's memory of the event is very
hazy, but he is convinced that it happened –

and that there are shady forces at work trying
to hush it up.

But WHY?

Faced with the usual firm denials from the
police, we come to the conclusion that this
episode was part of a secret police experiment
that went badly wrong. For years we have
been warning that the police are developing
new and sinister ways of fighting crime,
including the kind of robot we believe Mr
Winthrop encountered. We think this machine
malfunctioned and the police panicked.

Regular readers of this website will know that
we are convinced that the police routinely wipe
the memories of those that get too close to
uncovering the truth – this would explain Mr
Winthrop's hazy recollection.

Is there anyone else out there who can shed
any light on this incident? We want to hear
from YOU!

A SHORT TIME LATER,
ZAVONNE BRIEFS MAX
ON HIS SECOND TOP
SECRET MISSION . . .

MAX FLASH
MISSION 2
SUPERSONIC

Jonny Zucker

CENTRIFUGAL FORCE MACHINE

FLIGHT SIMULATOR

WEIGHTLESSNESS CHAMBER